Taped + trimmed pgs.
3/31/15 TB Fett

Heidi

Heidi

By Johanna Spyri
Adapted by Gail Herman
Illustrated by Lydia Halverson

A STEPPING STONE BOOK™

Random House 🏠 New York

Text copyright © 2011 by Gail Herman
Cover art and interior illustrations copyright © 2011 by Lydia Halverson

Visit us on the Web!
SteppingStonesBooks.com
www.randomhouse.com/kids

Educators and librarians, for a variety of teaching tools, visit us at
www.randomhouse.com/teachers

Library of Congress Cataloging-in-Publication Data
Herman, Gail.
Heidi / by Johanna Spyri ; adapted by Gail Herman ; illustrated by Lydia Halverson. — 1st ed.
p. cm.
"A Stepping Stone book."
Summary: A Swiss orphan is heartbroken when she must leave her beloved grandfather and their happy home in the mountains to go to school and to care for an invalid girl in the city.
ISBN 978-0-375-86899-3 (trade) — ISBN 978-0-375-96899-0 (lib. bdg.) — ISBN 978-0-375-89986-7 (ebook)
[1. Orphans—Fiction. 2. Grandfathers—Fiction. 3. Mountain life—Switzerland—Fiction. 4. Switzerland—History—19th century—Fiction.] I. Halverson, Lydia, ill. II. Spyri, Johanna, 1827–1901. Heidi. III. Title.
PZ7.H4315He 2011 [Fic]—dc22 2010045161

Printed in the United States of America

10 9 8 7 6 5 4 3 2 1

CONTENTS

I

UP THE
MOUNTAIN

One June morning, a small girl climbed a path
with her aunt. The path rose up through the
Alps, the mountains of Switzerland.

The child's cheeks were red. The sun was
hot, and she wore two dresses. A large red
scarf wound round her as well. It was easier to
wear the clothes than to carry them.

Halfway up the mountain, the woman and
child came to a village. The people of Dorfli
looked at them, curious.

"Wait! Detie!" one woman called to the aunt. "I'll come with you."

The girl sat down on the ground to wait.

"Tired, Heidi?" Detie asked.

"No, but I'm very hot," Heidi replied.

"Just keep going," her aunt said. "We'll be there before long."

Detie was taking Heidi all the way up the mountain. The little girl was an orphan. She'd been living with Detie since her parents died. But now Detie had a new job in Germany. Heidi was going to live with her grandfather.

Detie explained it all to the village woman when she joined them. "What?" said the woman. Her voice rose in surprise. "The girl will stay with Uncle Alp on the mountain?"

Everyone called Heidi's grandfather Uncle Alp, because he hardly ever came down the mountain. When he did, he scowled at the villagers. He held a great big walking stick. And he looked so wild.

The two women started to walk. Heidi trailed behind.

"You must be crazy!" the village woman whispered. "Everyone is afraid of Uncle Alp. He wants nothing to do with anyone!"

"He hasn't always been that way," Detie said.

Heidi didn't remember her grandfather any way at all. But when Uncle Alp was young, he had a great farm. Things were going fine, until he fell in with bad friends. He gambled and lost the land. Then he disappeared. Years later, he came back. He was raising a son alone and wanted help.

The villagers didn't trust him. But they liked the boy, Tobias. Tobias married Detie's sister, Adelheid. They settled down, and soon Heidi was born. Only two years later, Tobias was killed while building a house. Adelheid was so shocked that she died a few weeks after.

People blamed the old man. It was punishment for bad deeds, they said. That made him angry. He stopped talking and stayed on the mountain from that day on.

"Uncle Alp has to take Heidi!" Detie told the woman. "He is her grandfather! And I can't take her with me!"

As the women talked, Heidi fell farther and farther behind. The path twisted up the mountainside in a zigzag. She couldn't see Detie anymore, but she wasn't afraid. Heidi was only five, but she could already take care of herself.

A boy came up beside her. Peter, the goatherd, was climbing too. Heidi was glad for the company. She scrambled after him. But she was so bundled up! It made climbing hot, hard work.

Heidi didn't complain. Still, she thought Peter was very lucky. He wore comfortable clothes, and his feet were bare. He could step lightly over stones and bushes.

Suddenly, Heidi sat down. She pulled off her boots and stockings. She unwound the thick red scarf. Then she took off both dresses. Now she stood in nothing but a thin slip. Waving her bare arms, she smiled in delight.

Heidi placed her clothes in a neat pile. She felt so much happier! Free as air! She danced off to catch up with Peter.

"How many goats do you tend? Where do you take them? What do you do when you get there?" Heidi asked so many questions! She was curious about everything.

The climb was going quickly now. Soon they reached a hut midway between Dorfli and Uncle Alp's home.

This was Peter's house. It was small, brown, and run-down. It looked as if a strong wind would blow it over.

Peter was eleven, and spent very little time at home. But his mother and his grandmother rarely went out.

The village woman said good-bye to Detie and went into the hut to visit Grannie. Detie stopped as well, looking for Heidi.

"What a sight you are, Heidi!" Detie called in a shrill voice. "What have you done with your dresses? And your scarf? Where have you left all your clothes?"

Heidi pointed calmly down the mountain. "There they are," she said.

"Why on earth did you do that?" Detie asked.

"I didn't need them," Heidi told her. She nodded, thinking that explained it all.

"Peter, run back and get the clothes for me,"

Detie said. "And be quick about it. Don't just stand there!"

Peter stood with his hands in his pockets.

Finally, Detie said, "Look, here's something for you." She held out a bright new coin.

Peter dashed off, and was back with the clothes in no time. He tucked the coin away, smiling. Such riches didn't often come his way.

"Now carry the things up to Uncle's for me," Detie said.

It took another hour to reach Uncle Alp's hut. The little house looked out on a green valley. Three big fir trees stood behind it. Beyond the trees, mountaintops sparkled with snow.

Uncle Alp sat on a bench outside the hut. He had a pipe in his mouth and his hands on his knees. Heidi ran ahead of the others and went straight to him.

"Hallo, Grandfather," she said. And she held out her hand.

"Hey, what's that?" Uncle Alp stared at Heidi. Then he took her hand.

Heidi stared back. Her grandfather had a long beard and bushy gray eyebrows. She was fascinated!

"Here is Tobias's daughter," Detie told him. She came toward Heidi, with Peter right behind.

"Why have you brought her here?" Uncle Alp demanded. He turned to Peter. "And you, be off! Take your goats! And don't forget mine! You're already late."

The old man gave him such a look. Peter disappeared at once.

"Heidi has come to stay with you," Detie went on. She kept talking, explaining about her job.

The old man got up. Detie stepped back, frightened. But he only waved her away. "My turn, is it? Then go back where you came from. And don't come here again!"

"Good-bye, Heidi," Detie said quickly. She felt bad for the girl. How would Uncle Alp care for her? Still, she ran down the mountain, leaving Heidi behind.

2

AT GRANDFATHER'S

The old man sat down again. He stared at the ground in silence. Heidi didn't mind. She wanted to explore. She ran to the goat shed. Then she ran to the back of the house.

All at once, Heidi stopped. She turned her head, listening to the wind blow through the trees. When she came back to the front, Uncle Alp was still sitting on the bench.

Heidi came to stand beside him, hands behind her back. Finally, he looked up at her.

"What do you want to do now?" he asked.

"I want to see the inside of the hut," Heidi said. Her black eyes shone. She pointed to her bundle of clothes. "But I shan't want those. I want to be able to run like the goats."

"She's no fool," the old man muttered. "Still, bring the things inside," he told her.

Inside, Heidi saw that the hut was one big room. There were a table and a chair, and a bed in one corner. Opposite the bed were a stove and a pot. There was one cupboard for clothes, with shelves for food and plates.

It was so simple. Heidi liked it right away.

"Where shall I sleep, Grandfather?"

"Where you like."

Heidi was pleased. She climbed up a ladder to the hayloft. "I shall sleep up here! It's a splendid place."

Together, Heidi and her grandfather pushed

hay to make a bed and pillow. Uncle Alp used a heavy cloth for a sheet. He gave Heidi his own blanket.

"My whole bed is lovely!" said Heidi. "I wish it was bedtime now!"

"First, let us see about a meal," her grandfather said.

While Uncle Alp toasted cheese, Heidi laid

out plates and mugs. She found a big loaf of bread in the cupboard. Then she carried a small stool to the table.

"You know how to be helpful," Uncle Alp told her.

Heidi looked as happy as anyone could be.

After the meal, Uncle Alp busied himself around the hut. Heidi followed at his heels. Everything was new and interesting!

The afternoon passed quickly. A strong wind sprang up. It whistled and rustled through the fir trees. The sound pleased Heidi so much. She danced and jumped about.

Suddenly, she heard a shrill whistle. Peter had brought back the goats. Two went right up to Uncle Alp.

Heidi cried out with delight. Then she asked a rush of questions. "Are these ours, Grandfather? Where do they sleep? Will they always be here? What are their names?"

"The white goat is called Daisy. And the brown one is Dusky. Now I must see to them, and you must go to bed."

That night, the wind blew hard. It shook the whole hut and shrieked down the chimney.

Uncle Alp thought Heidi might be frightened. He climbed the ladder. Heidi was fast asleep, smiling.

A loud whistle woke Heidi. At first, she didn't know where she was. Then she heard her grandfather and Peter.

Heidi jumped out of bed. She splashed about in a tub of water. She ran outside, into the bright sunshine.

"Come here, general of the goats," Grandfather called to Peter. He dropped chunks of bread and cheese into Heidi's lunch bag. Peter watched with big eyes. It was twice the size of his own lunch.

"Now go up to the pasture with Peter and the goats," Uncle Alp said to Heidi.

On the mountain, the sun shone brightly. Flowers bloomed everywhere. The air smelled lovely. Heidi and Peter began to climb.

At one spot, Heidi rushed to and fro. She was so excited to see the primroses! She gathered flowers, stooping to put them in her apron.

"Heidi! Where have you got to?" Peter shouted.

"Here!" Heidi called from behind a small hill. She'd sat right down, enjoying the sweet smells.

"We've still a way to go!" Peter told her. Together, they kept climbing.

Finally, they rested at the foot of a rocky peak. Peter lay down in the sun to rest. Heidi sat beside him. Everything was very still. A gentle breeze set the flowers nodding.

The goats climbed about among the bushes. Heidi watched quietly, enjoying herself. Then one small white goat bleated sadly.

"What's the matter, Snowflake?" Heidi asked. She put her arms around its neck. Comforted, the goat stopped crying.

Heidi shared her bread and cheese with Peter. Peter nodded his thanks. To him, it was a feast!

Suddenly, Peter jumped up. A goat named Finch stood right at the edge of a steep dropoff. If the goat took one more step, it would fall right over the edge.

Peter caught hold of the goat. But then he slipped and fell. He couldn't get up without letting go, and the goat was struggling to get free.

"Heidi! Come and help!" Peter shouted.

Heidi saw at once what to do. She pulled up a handful of grass. Then she held it under Finch's nose.

"Come on," she said to the goat. "You don't want to fall and hurt yourself."

At that, the little goat turned. It stopped

struggling and ate the grass. Finally, Peter was able to stand. He took hold of the cord around Finch's neck. With Heidi pulling too, they brought the goat back to the others.

Peter raised a stick. He was going to beat the goat as punishment!

"Don't!" Heidi pleaded. "It will hurt him. Leave him alone!"

She looked at Peter so fiercely, he dropped the stick in surprise.

"I won't beat him," Peter said, "if you give me some cheese again tomorrow." That seemed fair to Peter.

Heidi agreed. "But you must never beat Finch or any other goat!"

It was getting late now. The setting sun spread a golden glow over the whole mountain. All at once, Heidi jumped up. "A fire!" she cried.

"Everything is on fire. The mountains! The snow! The sky!"

"It's always like this in the evening," Peter told her.

"Oh." Heidi sat back down. "How pretty!"

Slowly the color left. Everything turned gray. "It's all over," Heidi said, upset.

"It will be the same again tomorrow," explained Peter. "Now it's time to go home."

Back at the hut, Heidi told her grandfather all the wonderful things that had happened. "The fire was the best of all."

"It's the sun's way of saying good night," Uncle Alp told Heidi. "He spreads light so the mountains won't forget him. And then he comes back in the morning."

Heidi liked that idea very much. She fell asleep, dreaming of mountains and flowers and Snowflake and Finch.

3
A Visit to Grannie

All through the summer, Heidi went with Peter to the pasture. She grew strong and healthy. She felt as happy as a bird.

Then autumn came. Strong winds blew. "You must stay home now," Heidi's grandfather said. "Or you might be blown off the mountain."

Peter was disappointed, but Heidi was happy wherever she was. She watched her grandfather work, making cheese and building furniture.

She listened to the noise of the wind. It made music as it blew through the fir trees. The wind blew through her too. So she wore socks and shoes and a dress.

All at once, it turned very cold. One night it snowed. In the morning, everything was white.

The snow drifted higher and higher. The hut was buried up to the windows. Still, Peter kicked open the door to visit.

"Hullo," he said, pleased to be there. Snow trickled off him.

"Well, General," said Uncle Alp. "How are you, now that you have to leave your army and go to school?"

School? Heidi wanted to know all about it. She had so many questions. Peter explained about the schoolhouse, the lessons, the teacher, and the other students. By the time he finished, he was dry.

"I'll come again," Peter promised Heidi. "And Grannie says she would like you to come and see her."

Something new! Heidi was delighted. Every day she asked Uncle Alp if she could go. "No, the snow is too deep," he told her.

Finally, the snow froze hard. "Come on, then," the old man told Heidi. He dragged a big sled outside. Then he sat down with Heidi on his knees.

Suddenly, he pushed off. The sled sped down the mountainside. Heidi felt as though she were flying! She screamed with delight.

Just outside Peter's hut, they stopped. "Start for home when it gets dark," Uncle Alp said. Before anyone could see him, he turned to walk back up the mountain.

Heidi went inside. The place was small and cramped. Peter's mother sat at a table, sewing.

In a corner, an old woman worked at a spinning wheel.

Heidi went straight to her. "Here I am, Grannie."

Grannie raised her head. She felt for Heidi's hand. "Are you Heidi?"

"Yes." Heidi's sharp eyes missed nothing. "One of your shutters is loose," she said. "It might break a window."

"I can't see it, my dear," said Grannie. "But I can hear it—and everything else that creaks and clatters. The place is falling to pieces, I am afraid."

The old woman was scared and blind! Heidi was heartbroken.

"But it is so good to hear a friendly voice," Grannie went on. "And yours, I love already. Come sit beside me."

Feeling better, Heidi chattered away.

Suddenly, Peter burst into the room. He grinned at Heidi.

"Back from school already?" his mother said. "My, this afternoon passed so quickly. How is your reading?"

"Just the same," said Peter.

"I have a book of hymns," Grannie explained to Heidi. "I keep hoping Peter will read them to me. But he doesn't seem able to learn."

When Peter's mother lit a lamp, Heidi jumped up. It was time to go. She ran off so fast, no one could stop her. But there was Uncle Alp, coming to meet her. He wrapped Heidi in a sack and carried her home.

As soon as they were indoors, Heidi began to talk. She told Uncle Alp about the falling-down house. "We'll go and help Grannie tomorrow," she said. "Won't we?"

Uncle Alp agreed. The next day, while Heidi

visited, he hammered the shutter against the house. Peter's mother tried to thank him, but he brushed her away.

Each time Heidi visited, Uncle Alp went with her. He never spoke, but he always fixed something else. He couldn't fix Grannie's eyes, though. Heidi still felt bad about that. But Grannie told her that she didn't mind being blind. Not when Heidi was with her.

4
Two Unexpected Visitors

Another happy summer passed. Then Heidi's second winter was almost over too. The sun began to melt the snow.

Heidi was old enough to go to school now. But Uncle Alp did not plan to send her. Even when the church pastor from Dorfli visited, Uncle Alp would not listen.

"She's not a goat or a bird," the pastor told Uncle Alp. "It's high time she began to read and write. She must come to school."

"She can't go down the mountain in winter," said Uncle Alp.

"Come live in Dorfli, then. What sort of life do you lead up here?" asked the pastor.

"People in Dorfli hate me," Uncle Alp said. He shook hands with the pastor. "I know you mean well. But my decision is final. I won't send the child to school. And I won't live in the village."

That day brought another surprise visitor. Detie swept into the hut. She wore a brand-new hat with a feather. Uncle Alp looked her up and down in silence.

"I have a wonderful chance for Heidi," she said. "The family I work for has rich relatives in Frankfurt, Germany. They have a little girl who is in a wheelchair. She has lessons by herself with a tutor. It's terribly dull. She needs a playmate. I thought of Heidi! The housekeeper said that she would do."

Uncle Alp said, "It doesn't interest me."

Detie blew up like a rocket. She yelled and yelled. "I've heard you won't let her learn!" she finally said, and threatened to take Uncle Alp to court.

Uncle Alp didn't know what to do. "Take her, then!" he yelled back. He strode out of the hut.

"I'm not coming," Heidi told Detie.

"You heard your grandfather." Detie tried to talk in a sweet voice. "He wants you to go with me. If you don't like it, you can always come back."

"Could I come back again this evening?" Heidi asked.

Detie packed Heidi's clothes. "Well, no. It's too far for that." She caught Heidi's hand, and they set off down the mountain.

Peter passed them on the path. But Detie kept tight hold of Heidi and hurried on.

"She's taking Heidi away!" Peter cried. He rushed into his hut.

Grannie opened the window and called, "Don't take the child away from us!"

"That's Grannie!" Heidi tried to free her hand. "I want to see her!"

"No time!" huffed Detie. "We can't miss our train. When you come back, you can bring her a present. Something nice to eat. Maybe a nice, soft roll. One that's easy to chew."

"Yes!" said Heidi, excited now. Grannie would like that. "Can we get to Frankfurt today?"

5
A NEW LIFE
BEGINS

Detie took Heidi to the big house in Frankfurt. The owner, Mr. Sesemann, was wealthy. His wife had died long ago. His only child, Clara, spent all her days in a wheelchair.

Mr. Sesemann was often away on business. A housekeeper looked after Clara. Miss Rottenmeier, a disagreeable woman, was in charge of everything.

When Miss Rottenmeier opened the door, she stared at Heidi. "What's your name?"

Heidi told her. Miss Rottenmeier didn't believe her. "That can't be. What is your proper name?"

"I don't remember."

"That's no way to answer!" The housekeeper thought Heidi was being rude.

Detie stepped in. "She is named Adelheid, after her mother."

Miss Rottenmeier thought that was a little better. But she still wasn't happy with Heidi. Clara was twelve, and Heidi not yet eight. "How will you do lessons together?" she asked. "What books have you been using?"

"None," Heidi replied.

"What's that you say? How did you learn to read?" Miss Rottenmeier asked.

"I haven't learned to read," Heidi told her. "Nor has Peter."

"Good gracious me!" Miss Rottenmeier cried

in dismay. "What have you learned, then?"

Always honest, Heidi said, "Nothing."

Miss Rottenmeier turned to Detie. "Really! She won't do at all!"

But Detie was already running out of the house. Clara, who'd been watching all along, waved Heidi over. "Do you want to be called Heidi or Adelheid?" she asked.

"Everyone calls me Heidi."

"Well, I'll call you that too," Clara said. "It suits you. I've never seen anyone quite like you before. Have you always had short, curly hair?"

"Yes, I think so," Heidi said cheerfully.

"Are you glad to be here?" Clara continued.

"No, but I shall be going home soon," Heidi replied. "I'll have some nice rolls to give to Grannie too."

"You are a funny child." Clara smiled. She was very happy to have Heidi there. She told

Heidi about her lessons and her tutor, Mr. Usher.

When it was time for supper, a servant named Sebastian wheeled Clara to the fancy dining room. Heidi followed and sat at a long table set for three. Beside Heidi's plate was a soft white roll.

She could save it for Grannie! "May I have this?" she asked Sebastian.

The servant nodded. He held out a dish of baked fish.

"Am I to have some of that too?" Heidi asked, surprised.

"What a way to talk to servants!" Miss Rottenmeier exclaimed. "I will have to teach you manners, Adelheid."

The housekeeper gave instructions on how to act morning, noon, and night. She went on and on. At last, she ended the lecture. "Now, Adelheid, do you understand?"

Clara smiled and said, "Heidi's asleep."

Heidi awoke the next morning, confused. She was in a big room in a high white bed, so different from her own.

All at once, she remembered that she was

in Frankfurt. She dressed quickly. Then she went to the window to see outside. But the curtains were too heavy to open. And the windows were so high! She wouldn't be able to see out, anyway.

Heidi began to feel rather frightened. She ran from window to window, like a bird in a cage trying to find freedom.

Just then there was a tap at the door. "Breakfast is ready," a servant called.

Heidi didn't know what she was supposed to do. So she sat and waited.

After a while, Miss Rottenmeier bustled in. "Don't you even know what breakfast is?" she huffed. She led Heidi back to the dining room.

6

A Bad Day
for Rottenmeier

Later in the study, Clara and Heidi were waiting for the tutor. Clara asked Heidi about her life at home. Heidi chattered away about the mountains and goats and everything she loved so well. She didn't stop until Mr. Usher came to teach.

But even then, Heidi couldn't stop thinking about the fresh air and the trees and the sound of the wind.

Wait! Did she hear something? That lovely

music, when the wind rustled the fir-tree branches?

Without another thought, Heidi rushed across the room. She caught the tablecloth as she went by. Books and paper flew everywhere. Ink streamed over the floor.

Heidi didn't notice as she raced through the house. But the clatter echoed through the rooms. Miss Rottenmeier heard. She hurried after Heidi.

"Please don't punish her!" Clara called. "It was quite by accident!"

"The child is impossible!" Miss Rottenmeier muttered. "And where has she got to now?"

Heidi had stopped at last. She was standing by the front door, peering outside. "I heard the fir trees rustling. But I can't see them!" she said, confused.

"Fir trees indeed!" said Miss Rottenmeier.

"We're not in the woods here. Those were carriages rolling past. Now come see the mess you made. You must learn to sit still."

Heidi went back to the study and sat quietly for the lesson. But she didn't pay much attention. She was wondering about Frankfurt. Weren't there any trees here? She needed to talk to someone. She stopped Sebastian as he carried a big tray of dishes down the hall.

"What do you want, miss?" he asked crossly.

"I only want to ask a question. It's nothing naughty like this morning," she added. Heidi did feel terrible about the inky mess!

"All right," Sebastian said. He was much more pleasant now.

"Can you open a window?" Heidi asked.

"Of course," he said, and threw one open.

Heidi was too small to see out. So Sebastian brought over a stool. Heidi climbed right up.

After a quick glance outside, she turned away.

"There's nothing but stony streets," she said, disappointed. "What's on the other side of the house?"

"Nothing different," Sebastian replied.

The train had carried her far from mountains and pastures. It was hard for Heidi to understand.

"Where can I go to see the whole valley?" she asked Sebastian.

"Somewhere high up," Sebastian told her. "A church tower."

Not wasting an instant, Heidi ran out the front door. She walked on and on. People were in such a hurry!

She saw a boy standing on a corner. On his back he carried a hurdy-gurdy, an organ that played when he turned a crank. In his arms he held a tortoise.

"Can you take me to a church with a tower?" Heidi asked.

"Yes," the boy replied. "Will you give me two pennies?"

"I haven't got pennies," Heidi said, "but Clara does. She would give me some."

Heidi and the boy went off together. They followed a long street to the church. Heidi pulled a rope, and a bell rang.

The door opened with a creak. "Be off with you!" a man said to Heidi. "And don't try your tricks again!"

"Please let me climb the tower," she pleaded.

The church keeper looked down at Heidi. His frown faded. "Oh, well, come along."

Heidi and the man climbed up and up. The stairs grew narrow. At last, they reached the top.

The keeper lifted Heidi up to a window. But

still, there were no trees to be seen. Only roofs, chimneys, and towers.

Disappointed, Heidi said, "It isn't a bit what I expected!"

On the way down, Heidi stopped at a landing. A fat gray cat sat beside a basket. Little kittens tumbled inside.

"What darlings!" Heidi exclaimed.

"Would you like one?" the keeper asked. "Indeed, you can have them all."

"Oh! Clara will be pleased!" said Heidi. She described the big house. The keeper said he would bring them over.

First, though, Heidi chose two kittens. She put a white one and a tabby in her pockets. Then the hurdy-gurdy boy led her back to the house.

"Come in quickly!" cried Sebastian when he saw Heidi. He slammed the door behind her. He didn't notice the boy at all. "Miss Rottenmeier and Clara are already at the table!"

Heidi rushed into the dining room. There was an awful silence.

"How naughty to leave the house!" the housekeeper finally said.

"Meow," came the reply.

"How dare you make fun of me!" Miss Rottenmeier said.

"I didn't," Heidi said.

"Meow, meow."

The housekeeper almost choked with anger. "Leave the room," she ordered.

Heidi tried to explain. But the kittens meowed again.

"Why do you keep doing that?" Clara asked. "Can't you see Miss Rottenmeier is angry?"

"It's not me. It's the kittens," Heidi finally got out.

"What?" Miss Rottenmeier screamed. "Kittens? Here? Get rid of them!" She rushed out of the room, terrified of the tiny cats.

Clara took the kittens onto her lap. "Sebastian, help us," she said. "Find a corner for the kittens. A place Miss Rottenmeier won't see."

The next morning, the doorbell rang. It was the hurdy-gurdy boy and his tortoise.

"Clara owes me money," the boy told Sebastian. He described how he had met Heidi. Then he followed Sebastian to the study. Heidi and Clara were having their lesson with Mr. Usher.

In moments, the boy was playing music for them. Miss Rottenmeier rushed to the study.

"Stop that at once!" The housekeeper darted toward the boy. But she tripped over something on the floor. The tortoise!

Miss Rottenmeier leaped and screamed. Finally, she collapsed in a chair.

The boy snatched up the tortoise as Sebastian led him away. "Here's the money from Miss Clara, and a bit more," he told the boy.

In the study, Mr. Usher tried to start the

lesson again. This time, Miss Rottenmeier stayed close by, keeing watch. But Sebastian soon returned. He held a big basket for Clara.

"For me?" said Clara, surprised.

Suddenly, the blankets in the basket parted. The kittens jumped out, one after another. They rushed madly about. The room was in an uproar.

Miss Rottenmeier froze, unable to speak. At last, Heidi gathered the kittens, and Sebastian brought them to the corner where the other two were.

Clara smiled happily. She had enjoyed her lesson.

7

GRANDMAMMA'S VISIT

The next few days passed quietly. Heidi was growing more and more homesick. She wasn't learning her letters. She couldn't go outdoors. After dinner, she'd sit alone in her room. There, she'd think about the mountain. She could hardly bear it!

Then Heidi remembered what Detie had said: She could always go back to Grandfather if she wanted. So one afternoon, she gathered all the rolls she'd been saving for Grannie. She put on her old straw hat and went to the front door.

Miss Rottenmeier was just coming in. "What does this mean?" she demanded.

"I want to go home to see Grandfather and Grannie," Heidi said.

"You're an ungrateful girl!" Miss Rottenmeier said, and sent Heidi to her room.

Miss Rottenmeier followed close behind Heidi. "You look like a beggar's child," she said. She was determined to get rid of Heidi's hat and the rest of her old clothes. She saw the stale rolls Heidi had collected.

"Throw everything in the dustbin!" she ordered Sebastian.

"Oh no!" Heidi wailed to Clara. "I must keep my hat. And now Grannie won't get any nice bread!"

"Heidi, don't cry," Clara begged. "I promise

to get you just as many rolls as you saved. Or even more! You can take them to Grannie when you go home."

Still, Heidi couldn't stop crying. That night, she went to bed with red eyes. And there, under the quilt, was her old straw hat. Sebastian had saved it!

A few days later, Clara's father, Mr. Sesemann, came home. The first thing he did was see his daughter. Heidi was with her.

"So this is our little Swiss girl," Mr. Sesemann said in a friendly way. He could see how happy she made Clara.

"Clara is always good to me," Heidi told him.

But Miss Rottenmeier couldn't stop complaining. "You should see the sort of people she brings here! And the animals!"

Mr. Sesemann shook his head. "Please don't

see Heidi's funny ways as faults. Make sure to treat her kindly."

He stayed only two weeks. But more family was coming: Clara's grandmother.

"You must call her Gracious Madam," Miss Rottenmeier told Heidi. "Not Grandmamma, as Clara does."

"Gracious Madam." Heidi repeated the words again and again. She wanted to get them right. But was that the right order? Surely "Madam" must come first.

Soon Clara's grandmother's carriage rolled up to the house. Heidi was called from her room to meet her.

"Good evening, Madam Gracious," she said.

The old woman laughed. "Is that what you say in the mountains?"

"No. No one is called that at home," said Heidi.

"Nor here either. I'm always Grandmamma. And you shall call me that as well."

Grandmamma had such a kind look. Heidi loved her at once.

Grandmamma liked Heidi too. She asked her to visit in her room. Then she showed Heidi a storybook with pictures in it.

One page showed a meadow, with a shepherd and animals. It reminded Heidi of home. She burst into tears.

Grandmamma let Heidi cry. When she grew calm, she asked Heidi, "And how are your lessons?"

"I haven't learned a thing!" Heidi admitted. "But I knew I wouldn't. It's too hard to read. Peter said so. And he's tried and tried."

"Listen to me, Heidi." Grandmamma looked her in the eye. "You believed Peter, and so you never learned. Now you must believe me. Try

hard, and pay attention to Mr. Usher. In a little while, you will be able to read quite well. And then you shall have this book!"

Heidi listened with shining eyes. "I wish I could read right now!"

8

HOMESICKNESS

Even with Grandmamma visiting, Heidi's heart felt heavy. At night, she lay awake. She grew pale and thin. More than ever, she missed home.

Heidi understood she couldn't leave just because she wanted to. She didn't want the Sesemann family to think she was ungrateful. So she tried to keep her sadness inside.

When she could fall asleep, she would dream of the mountains. But then she'd wake and find herself still in the big bed in Frankfurt. She would cry into her pillow so no one would hear.

Still, Grandmamma knew Heidi wasn't happy.

"Do you know how to pray, Heidi?" she asked. "When you are sad, it is a comfort to tell God. He can find a way to make you happy."

Heidi brightened. She ran to her room. She prayed that she would get to go home.

A week later, Heidi was able to read. She was very excited. The black letters came alive and turned into stories. And just as Grandmamma had promised, the picture book was hers.

The shepherd story was Heidi's favorite. Now she knew what it was really about: A young shepherd is happy at home. But he leaves for another farm, even though it angers his father. The new farm is dreary. In the end, he returns home. All is forgiven, and the father and son are happy again.

Time passed. One day, Grandmamma asked Heidi, "Are you still troubled?"

Heidi nodded. "God didn't hear me. Nothing has happened."

"If we ask for something that isn't quite right," Grandmamma said, "he won't give it to us. But if we trust in him, he'll find us something better."

Heidi listened very carefully. She wouldn't give up, she decided. Heidi trusted Grandmamma and cared for her greatly.

When it came time for Grandmamma to leave, the house felt quiet and empty.

Autumn and winter passed. Strange things began to happen in the Frankfurt house. Each morning, servants found the front door open. They searched the home. But nothing was ever stolen.

They tried double-locking the door. Still, it was wide open in the mornings.

One servant said he'd seen a white figure on the stairs after dark. Then it vanished. It had to be a ghost!

When Clara heard, she cried, "Papa must come home!"

Two days later, Mr. Sesemann stood at his front door.

Before he did anything else, Mr. Sesemann sent a message to his friend Dr. Classen. "Say it is serious," he told Sebastian. "And that he should spend the night."

The doctor came right away. "You look pretty well," Dr. Classen told Clara's father.

"Your attention *is* needed, but not by me.

We've a ghost!" Mr. Sesemann explained it could all be a joke. Or a burglar. In any case, they'd need to keep watch.

The two friends sat in the room by the entrance of the house. They chatted for hours. Outside, everything grew quiet.

Suddenly, they heard a noise. The bolt was pushed. Then a key turned. The men rushed to the door.

Moonlight streaked the hall. They could see a white figure standing still.

"Who's there?" shouted the doctor.

The figure turned and cried out. It was Heidi, in her white nightgown.

"What are you doing here, child?" asked Mr. Sesemann.

Heidi trembled. "I don't know," she said in a small voice.

"I think this is a case for me," the doctor

said. He led Heidi gently back to her bed.

"I didn't know I'd gone downstairs," Heidi whispered. "I was just there. Every night I dream I'm back with Grandfather. I hear the wind. I get up and open the door. It's so beautiful! But when I wake up, I'm still in Frankfurt."

"Do you like Frankfurt?" Dr. Classen asked.

Heidi said, "Yes." But it sounded like she meant "No."

"Wasn't the mountain dull?" the doctor asked.

"Oh no! It was wonderful!" Heidi got no further. Tears rained down her cheeks.

The doctor patted her hand. "Have a good cry. Then go to sleep. In the morning, everything will be all right."

Dr. Classen went to find Mr. Sesemann. "The child has been sleepwalking," he explained. "She's terribly homesick, and very upset. Why, she's skin and bones! There's only one cure. She should leave for home tomorrow."

Clara's father agreed.

9

HOME AGAIN

The next morning, Clara tried to change her father's mind. She would miss Heidi!

"Heidi's health is poor," Mr. Sesemann told her gently. "She might sleepwalk up to the roof. We can't risk that."

Meanwhile, Heidi waited in her room. "I do believe nobody's told you!" Mr. Sesemann said as he came in. "You're going home today! Are you pleased?"

"Home!" Heidi gasped. The color came into

her cheeks. "Oh yes, I am pleased!"

She and Clara had to say good-bye quickly. "Take this!" Clara held up a basket of rolls.

"Thank you for everything," Heidi told Mr. Sesemann. She stepped up into the carriage. "And please thank the doctor too."

Sebastian went with Heidi on the long train trip. Then he found her a ride up to Dorfli on a cart.

All the while, Heidi wore her old straw hat. She held the basket of rolls, along with a package for her grandfather.

"Thank you," Heidi told the driver when he stopped. She raced uphill. *Will Grannie be sitting by her spinning wheel?* she wondered.

Up ahead, Heidi saw Peter's hut. She flew into the room, out of breath.

"Goodness me!" A voice came from the corner. "That was how Heidi used to come in."

"It *is* Heidi, Grannie!" Heidi threw herself into the old woman's lap. "I'll never go away again! And you won't have to eat hard rolls."

The old woman cried tears of joy. "You're the best present of all," she told Heidi.

Heidi promised to see Grannie the next day. Then she went up the mountain. Everything seemed so beautiful! The snowy peaks. The green pastures. Little pink clouds in the sky.

Soon Heidi saw the fir trees . . . then the hut . . . then Grandfather sitting on the bench outside.

Heidi flung her arms around him. "Grandfather! Grandfather!"

Uncle Alp's eyes grew wet with tears. "So you've come back, Heidi."

Heidi told him everything and gave him the package. Inside was a letter from Mr. Sesemann, along with money. Uncle Alp read the letter. "The money is for you," he said.

"I don't need it," Heidi said. Now that she was home, she had everything she wanted.

Then she heard a shrill whistle. It was Peter, tending the goats. Heidi ran toward him. The goats crowded round.

"I'm glad you're back!" Peter told Heidi.

The next day, Heidi went to see Grannie. "The rolls taste so good!" the old woman told her. "I feel better already!"

Heidi beamed. Suddenly, she knew what she could do with the money. "I'll get more rolls from the baker in Dorfli!" she told Grannie.

She sang and danced around the room with joy. Then Heidi caught sight of Grannie's hymnbook. "I can read now too," she said.

She stood on a stool to get the book. "Here's one about the sun," she said, turning the pages.

The golden sun
His course doth run,
And spreads his light,
So warm and bright,
Upon us all.

After, Grannie sighed. "Oh, that's done me so much good," she told Heidi.

Heidi chattered more to Grannie. She chattered to her grandfather too, as they climbed up the mountain later.

"If God had let me come home right away," she told him, "Grannie would only have a few rolls. And I wouldn't be able to read. But God waited for the right time."

The old man walked on in silence, thinking. He stayed quiet later while Heidi read out loud from her picture book. It was the story about the young shepherd. Uncle Alp listened very carefully to the part about forgiveness.

That night Uncle Alp gazed at Heidi, sleeping. He made a decision.

The next morning, he called out, "We'll go to church together."

They'd never done that before! Minutes later, they set off down the steep path.

At the end of the service, Uncle Alp took Heidi to see the pastor.

"You were right," Uncle Alp told him. "Heidi should go to school. We'll move to Dorfli for the winter."

The pastor grasped his hand. "And I shall welcome you!"

All around them, people whispered, "Uncle Alp is really so gentle with the girl! He's not a bad lot at all!"

10

A VISITOR
FOR HEIDI

That spring, Heidi received a letter from Frankfurt. Clara had written, saying she would visit in the summer. Now Heidi was expecting her any day. Finally, one morning, she saw the doctor climb up the mountain. Clara must be with him!

Heidi rushed over. "Thank you again a thousand times for sending me to Grandfather!" she cried.

Dr. Classen explained he was there in Clara's

place. Heidi's friend was feeling too poorly to visit. But she planned to visit the following spring.

Heidi was so disappointed! Still, the good doctor was there. Heidi didn't know he'd just lost a child and was alone now. But she did know he had a lonely look.

So she took his hand. Immediately, his face brightened. They went into the hut to see Uncle Alp. Then Dr. Classen opened a large package he'd brought.

When everything had been spread out, Heidi stared in amazement. There were so many presents—even some for Peter and his family.

Heidi carried those down the mountain. Coffee cakes! A giant sausage! And a shawl to keep Grannie warm.

Each morning after that, Dr. Classen went

with Heidi and Peter and the goats. Peter didn't like this very much. Heidi hardly looked his way at all! But there was extra food now, so it was all right in the end.

Heidi thought the doctor still looked sad, though. She remembered how she felt in Frankfurt. "I think you have to wait," she told him. "Maybe God has something good to give you out of this sadness. You have to be patient."

All that month, the weather was fine. When the last day of September came, the doctor's holiday was over.

"I wish I could take you back with me," he told Heidi. There were tears in his eyes as he turned to leave.

Heidi felt miserable. "Doctor!" she sobbed. "I will come with you!"

The doctor put his hand on her shoulder.

"No. You must stay here with your grandfather. But if I am ever ill, will you take care of me?"

"Oh yes!" Heidi promised him. "I love you nearly as much as Grandfather!"

II

WINTER
IN DORFLI

That winter, the snow lay deep on the mountain. Heidi, Uncle Alp, and their goats were already living in the village.

Heidi liked their new home very much. Her bed was in a cozy corner, right near a warm stove. There was so much to do! Heidi went to school and worked hard.

Peter, though, was hardly ever there—even when he could make it down the mountain and into town.

"You weren't at school," Heidi told him one afternoon.

"You deserted your post, General," Uncle Alp said to Peter. "What would you do if your goats ran away?"

"Punish them," Peter replied. "They'd deserve it."

"Then listen to me, General," Uncle Alp said. "If you don't go to school, I'll give you what you deserve."

Peter thought hard as he and Heidi walked up to his hut. Heidi skipped beside him, chattering away. She told Peter how Dusky and Daisy had refused to eat in their new home. They just stood quietly, with drooping heads.

"Grandfather said they were feeling like I did in Frankfurt," Heidi said. "They'd never left the pasture before. Can you imagine leaving home, Peter?"

Peter wasn't listening. He was thinking about what Uncle Alp had told him. "I'll go to school!" Peter said.

Heidi was glad about that. But she felt upset when she saw Grannie. The old woman lay sick in bed. She was wrapped in her new warm shawl. Still, the bed was hard and her pillow thin.

"Are you very ill, Grannie?" Heidi asked. She stood close beside her.

The old woman stroked her arm. "It's only the frost. It's gotten into my old, old bones."

"Your bed slopes down at the head," Heidi observed. "That's not right." She couldn't help but think about her bed in Frankfurt. If only Grannie could sleep in a bed like that!

"I have much to be thankful for," Grannie said. "The lovely rolls. The fine shawl. And you. Will you read to me today?"

Heidi read several hymns. A happy look spread over Grannie's face. "When you come and read, I'm comforted," she told Heidi.

That night, in her own cozy bed, Heidi thought about Grannie. Heidi wouldn't be able to visit much in the winter. She was in Dorfli, and Grannie up the mountainside. The snow would make it difficult. How could Grannie hear her hymns?

Heidi wondered what could be done. Suddenly, she had an idea. She felt so pleased, she could hardly wait for morning.

The next day, Peter went to school right on time. After, he went with Heidi to her house.

"You must learn to read," Heidi told him.

"Can't be done," Peter replied quickly.

"I don't believe that," Heidi told him. "Grandmamma told me it wasn't so. And she was right. I'll teach you. Then you can read to Grannie every day."

"Not me," Peter growled.

Heidi frowned. Her black eyes flashed. Peter needed to listen to her!

"I'll tell you what will happen if you don't learn," she said. "You will go to school in Frankfurt, in a great big building. You'll stay there till you've grown up. And everyone will make fun of you because you can't read."

It sounded horrible. "All right. I'll do it," Peter agreed.

Once again, Heidi was all smiles. "We'll start now." She opened an alphabet book and read: "'If *A, B, C* you do not know, before the judge you'll have to go.'"

"I won't go to the judge," Peter mumbled.

"Then hurry up and learn, so you won't have to," Heidi said.

Peter would try his hardest! He'd learn to read! Slowly he repeated the rhyme. He studied the letters *A, B, C* until he knew them.

"I'll read you the rest of the rhymes," Heidi told Peter. "Then you'll know what to expect."

"'If *D, E, F* you cannot say, bad luck is sure to come your way.'"

Heidi recited more letter rhymes.

Then she read, "'Trouble will be in store for you, if you can't say *N, O, P, Q.*'"

Peter stared at her in dismay. "All these threats!" he exclaimed.

Heidi's tender heart melted.

"Don't worry," she told him. "Just come every evening. If you go on like today, you'll know all your letters. Then nothing will happen to you!"

Day by day, letter by letter, they made their way through the alphabet.

Snow fell again. Heidi couldn't leave Dorfli. She couldn't visit Grannie. She felt so anxious! But by then, Peter could read.

"I am to read hymns to you now," he said to Grannie one afternoon. "Heidi told me to."

His mother fetched the book. Peter sat down at the table. He began to read.

"Well, would you believe it!" his mother said. Grannie just listened closely.

The next day at school, the class had a reading lesson.

"Should I pass over you?" the teacher asked Peter. "Or will you try to pick out a word or two?"

Peter took the book. He read three lines without one mistake.

"I'd almost given up on you!" the teacher

said. "But you've learned to read! How did this happen?"

"It was Heidi," Peter replied.

The teacher glanced at Heidi. But she was pretending not to listen, gazing off into space.

"And now you never miss school," the teacher went on. "Why is that?"

"Because of Uncle Alp," was the answer.

Soon everyone knew. Heidi and Uncle Alp were making good things happen.

12

MORE VISITORS

The winter passed. Soon it was May. The mountainsides were green. Flowers opened their petals. Heidi and her grandfather were back on the mountain.

A letter came from Clara. She and Grand-mamma were coming to visit.

Heidi was overjoyed. But Peter did not like the idea of more visitors. He told Grannie. She worried that these friends would take Heidi away.

Grannie was feeling better now. She was in her corner, spinning, when Heidi rushed in to talk about her Frankfurt friends. The more she talked, the more Grannie thought she would be leaving.

All of a sudden, Heidi stopped short. "What's the matter, Grannie? Aren't you pleased?"

"Yes." Grannie tried to smile. "I'm glad for your sake." Quickly, she changed the subject and asked Heidi to read.

Then one morning in June, Heidi gave a shout. A line of people was coming up the mountain.

First came two men, carrying Clara on a chair. Next, Grandmamma rode on horseback. Behind them came two more men. One pushed an empty wheelchair. The other carried a bundle of rugs and blankets.

Heidi sped over to hug Clara. Then she greeted Grandmamma.

"My dear uncle," Grandmamma said to Uncle Alp. "What a magnificent place!"

"It's heavenly." Clara sighed.

Uncle Alp lifted Clara ever so gently and placed her in the wheelchair. "This is more comfortable," he said kindly.

Clara could not stop looking around. "Wait till you see the flowers up in the pasture," Heidi told her.

Before long, Uncle Alp had set a table outside.

"Look!" Grandmamma said as they ate. "Clara is having a second piece of toast!" Normally, Clara would not even finish one.

"It's our mountain air," said Uncle Alp. He carried Clara up to Heidi's room.

"What a lovely place to sleep!" she cried.

"Suppose you leave Clara with us?" Uncle Alp suggested. "I'm sure she'd grow stronger. With all your rugs, I can make her a comfortable bed. And I promise to look after her."

It was decided. Clara would stay for a month. And Grandmamma would visit often.

The sights! The sounds! Clara thought it was all lovely. At bedtime, Heidi was asleep in no time. But Clara lay awake. From the hayloft window, she could see straight out into the sky.

It was a beautiful summer. Day after day, the sun shone. In the evening, the mountain peaks were a blaze of colors.

Clara did not want to miss a single moment. She sniffed the cool mountain air. She felt the warm sunshine. She stayed outdoors until it was dark. She drank big bowls of goat's milk and ate thick bread with butter and cheese. "I wish I could stay here forever," she told Heidi.

After two weeks, Uncle Alp asked Clara, "Won't you try and stand for a minute?"

He asked so gently. Clara did try, but she gave up quickly and clung to him. But each day he would ask. And each day she'd try for a little longer.

Then one day, Uncle Alp agreed to take Heidi and Clara up to the pasture. At last, Clara could see those beautiful flowers.

"Peter!" Heidi called out later. "We're coming with you tomorrow."

Peter growled like a bear. Heidi was finally coming to tend the goats with him. But she was taking that stranger!

13

THE UNEXPECTED
HAPPENS

At sunrise, Peter brought the goats to the hut. He was feeling cross. He glared at Clara's wheelchair. In a burst of rage, he gave it a shove.

The chair rolled down the slope and plunged out of sight. *Now that horrid girl will go away,* Peter thought. Everything would be as before. Then he left.

Heidi and Uncle Alp soon discovered the

chair was in bits. Uncle Alp thought that was curious. The chair couldn't have rolled like that on its own.

"We can go up, anyway," he told the girls. "I'll carry Clara."

Before long Heidi and Clara were settled on a blanket in the pasture. It was so delightful. Clara had an idea now what it meant to be well.

"We must go up to the meadow," Heidi told her. "That's where the flowers are." She called Peter to help.

Peter was feeling anxious. He knew he'd done a dreadful thing. He'd be sure to be found out. So he helped without grumbling.

They each took one of Clara's arms. At first, Clara flopped between them. "Put one foot down firmly," Heidi suggested. "It will hurt less."

Clara tried it. "You're right!" she cried

joyfully. "That didn't hurt nearly so much!"

Clara took more steps. She still held on to Heidi and Peter. But she grew steadier on her feet.

Heidi was wild with excitement. "Now we can come up every day! You'll never have to be in a wheelchair again!"

Each day after that, Clara practiced her walking. Each day she thought, *I am well! I can walk!* And she would go a little farther.

14
GOOD-BYE FOR THE PRESENT!

One morning, Grandmamma rode up the mountain. Heidi and Clara were sitting outside. First Heidi got up. Then so did Clara.

"Why, Clara!" Half laughing, half crying, Grandmamma hugged both girls.

"I must get word to your father," she told Clara. She wrote a note, and Uncle Alp whistled for Peter to bring it to Dorfli. "He will have the greatest surprise!" Grandmamma said.

Peter set off at once. But Mr. Sesemann was

planning his own surprise. He was climbing up the mountain to visit.

"Does this path lead to Heidi's hut?" he called out to Peter.

It's a policeman! Peter thought in a panic. *He's coming to get me because of the chair!* He dashed away.

"How shy he is!" Mr. Sesemann said. He trudged on.

Finally, he saw the hut—and two girls walking toward him. One was tall and fair. "Clara!" he shouted. "Can I believe my eyes?"

Everyone talked and laughed. Grandmamma gazed around with joy. Then her eyes fell on a bouquet of blue flowers. They were placed between low branches of a fir tree.

"Did someone bring them here for me?" she asked.

A scuffling sound came from behind the

trees. It was Peter, trying to sneak up the mountain.

"Come here!" she called. "Did you do this?"

"Yes," Peter said. He thought Grandmamma meant the wheelchair. "It's all broken."

"Broken?" Now Grandmamma was confused. But Uncle Alp quietly explained. Peter was responsible for the chair. He was expecting to be punished.

Grandmamma understood. "Poor boy," she said to Uncle Alp. "He's been punished already. Here we are, keeping Heidi away from him. We are all foolish when we are angry."

She turned to Peter. "We have a watchman inside us," she explained. "He sleeps until we do something wrong. Then he wakes up. He reminds us someone will find out and we'll get in trouble. But you helped Clara. Without her chair, she tried to walk. It's you who suffered."

Peter nodded.

"Then we'll say no more," said Grand-mamma. She decided to give Peter a present to remember them by. A penny a week.

Peter looked at her, wide-eyed. "Forever?" He thanked her and ran up the mountain. His troubles were over!

Mr. Sesemann wanted to give something to Uncle Alp too.

"I want nothing," Uncle Alp told him. "But please promise me one thing. Take care of Heidi. I will have nothing to leave her when I die."

"Heidi is like one of my family," Mr. Sesemann replied. "I will always provide for her. And Dr. Classen will as well. He is planning to live nearby. He loves her too."

"And now," Grandmamma said to Heidi. "Have you a wish?"

"Yes," said Heidi. "I would like Grannie to have my bed from Frankfurt."

"It shall be done!" Grandmamma said.

Heidi skipped off to tell Grannie. Everyone followed. Peter's mother saw them coming down the mountain. "They're all going home," she told Grannie.

"Oh dear." Grannie sighed. "Heidi must be going with them."

Just then Heidi flung open the door. "You will have a new bed, Grannie!" she said. "With three big pillows and a warm quilt! Grandmamma is sending it!"

Grannie smiled sadly. "She's very kind. I should be glad you are going with her. But I will be so unhappy without you."

"What's that?" Grandmamma said as she came inside. "Heidi is staying here. There is no question about that. She is such a comfort to you! And we shall come back every year to visit. To see Heidi, of course, and also to give thanks for Clara's health."

Heidi hugged everyone. "Hasn't everything turned out finely?" she cried.

And everyone agreed that yes, it had.

ABOUT THE AUTHOR

Johanna Spyri was born Johanna Louise Heusser in 1827 in Hirzel, Switzerland. As a child, she often spent summers in the Swiss Alps. After marrying Bernhard Spyri in 1852, she began to write. She published more than fifty stories for adults and children over her lifetime. She was also very dedicated to charitable causes. She had one son. Spyri died in 1901 and is buried in Zurich. Her face has appeared on a postage stamp and a coin in Switzerland.

If you liked

Heidi

you won't want to miss these stories!

Mary Lennox has heard stories of a locked,
deserted garden somewhere on her
uncle's land. Will she be able to find
the magic of the secret garden?

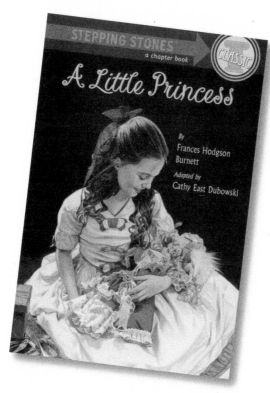

First Sara Crewe was a rich girl,
a little princess. Now she's an orphan
living in a cold attic. But with the help of
a mysterious friend, her life will change
in ways she never dreamed.